COLD SWEAT
Stories

Written
In Honor of Grandpa Chas' Birthday
(unfortunately he cannot remember how old he is)

by

PETER LINZMEYER

Illustrated by

THOMAS LINZMEYER

ISBN: 979-8-88640-259-9 (sc)
ISBN: 979-8-88640-260-5 (hc)
ISBN: 979-8-88640-261-2 (e)

THE EWINGS PUBLISHING

One Galleria Blvd., Suite 1900, Metairie, LA 70001
1-888-421-2397

Dedicated to

"Bud" Linzmeyer

(1909-1989)

and

"Bea" Linzmeyer

(1911-2007)

"...their inspiration remains with us today."

The CUCKOO CLOCK

n the early 1950s, that is, in the olden days, Chas Lingoober was about seven and one-half years old. He was skinny as a bean and so short that his Dad said he was "knee-high to a grass-hopper". After that comment by his Dad, Chas hunted down and snatched a grass-hopper resting peacefully, and minding its own business, on the stem of a tiger lily in the backyard of the Lingoober home.

He stomped down on the hopper and crushed it flatter than a pancake. After doing a wide-eyed examination of the dead bug and its squished juicy inner parts and greenish colored totally flattened legs, Chas decided with an air of relief that he was taller than the grasshopper's knees.

Of greater interest to Chas than the recently deceased and very squished grass-hopper was the front hall of the Lingoober home. This place was called the "front" hall to distinguish it from another hall called the "back" hall. This front hall featured dark red, somewhat spotted and slightly worn carpet, sea-foam green wallpaper with a floral pattern and a half-way elaborate overhead light fixture from the 1920's shaped like a wine carafe. The light was turned on by pushing an old fashioned button and a similar operation was required to turn it off. Chas delighted in turning the front hall light on and off by repeatedly pushing those old fashioned on and off buttons. His button pushing was accompanied by a loud clicking sound as the switch turned the light on or off.

Despite having been forbidden to play with the light switch buttons, Chas still engaged in this forbidden activity at least two or three times a day, just as he had been doing, and had been told not to do, since he was five years old. The front hall was special in that it had multiple doors including one double door to the Lingoober living room, another double door to the Lingoober dining room which in turn had a swinging door leading to the Lingoober kitchen, and a third door that opened to another smaller room where hats, coats and umbrellas where parked and which in turn showed off the inside of the front door of the Lingoober home.

Not to be omitted from this front hall description were the stairs which lead from the front hall to the second floor of the Lingoober house. On one side of the stairs was a wall with the same sea-foam green wall paper that covered the walls of the front hall. On the other side of the stairs was a banister, more commonly called a handrail, resting on spokes attached to each step. It was great fun to ride on the banister from the top of the stairs all the way down to the bottom. Of course, this activity was also forbidden, which did not prevent Chas from sliding down the banister almost as often as he goofed around with the buttons on the light switch. The reason why sliding down the banister was not allowed had nothing to do with Chas, who was a professional banister slider, but it had a lot to do with his older sister, Betty. One day, she tried sliding down the bannister and landed on her head on the red carpeted floor of the front hall.

She wailed so long and so pathetically, one would have thought that she had fallen out of a third story window. In any event, the wailing produced the absolute and stern order from their Dad to stay off the banister. The penalty for being caught on the banister was banishment to the culprit's bedroom, without dinner. Of course, Chas was smart enough not to get caught.

One time, after a banister thrill ride, his sister, Betty, the same sister who fell off the banister and bumped her head and cried so pathetically, threatened to report Chas' banister misdeed to their Dad. Chas told her that if she did so, he would stuff her favourite doll in the toilet and put a dead mouse in her bed. After receiving those threats, which were accompanied by menacing gestures by her younger brother, Betty decided not to report anything to anybody.

In addition to the light switch buttons and the banister on the stairs, both of which were off-limits for Chas, there was a fascinating thing hanging on the front hall wall, immediately to the left of the large door that opened to the coat and hat and umbrella room. That thing was a cuckoo clock. His Mom said that the clock was made in the Black Forest area of Germany and was given to her in 1938 by Aunt Edna as a wedding gift. Today was not going to be a good day for either the cuckoo clock or for Chas. As a matter of fact, it was a particularly bad day for both.

To understand how bad it was, it is important to know something about his Mom's clock hanging on the front hall wall. That clock was in the shape of a small wooden Swiss chalet and decorated with a lot of dark chocolate coloured wooden leaves. It did not look like a German chalet, probably because there is no such thing as a German chalet. The face of the clock with numbers from 1 to 12 was located on the ground floor of this little wall house. In its upper floor, there was an intriguing trap door which was supposed to open when the clock hands arrived at each hour. Out of the trap door a small yellow and green cuckoo bird was supposed to pop and then peep whatever number of hours the clock hands indicated.

Actually, this cuckoo clock did not work quite right, because the cuckoo bird popped out of its house to announce the time twelve minutes past the hour, rather than on the hour. The cuckoo bird was unable to peep, instead it squeaked in an annoying manner the number of hours, always twelve minutes late. So, when the yellow and green bird squeaked three times, you would know that it was twelve minutes past three, either in the afternoon or late at night.

Chas' Dad made some comment about the Germans not knowing how to build a clock that worked properly. He suggested to Chas' Mom that she should ask Aunt Edna for a replacement clock, perhaps one of an electric variety and made in America, a suggestion which his Mom thought was outrageous.

She told him that the not very beautiful chartreuse plastic lamp with the false Tiffany shade received as a wedding gift from Dad's sister, Bernice, known affectionately as "Aunt Berna", should be sent back to Berna for replacement. But what Chas' Dad thought about the cuckoo clock or what Chas' Mom thought about the plastic lamp from Aunt Berna had very little to do with the following events. Under the cuckoo clock house hung two sets of chains. Attached to each chain was a bronze weight in the shape of a pine cone. The weights somehow made the clock work as they slowly sank towards the red carpeted floor. The weights had to be pulled up to the underside of the wooden chalet once every three or four days. As soon as they were up there, they began again to make their way slowly, ever so slowly, towards the floor. Whenever visitors came to the Lingoober house, Chas' Mom would point out the cuckoo clock located so prominently on the sea foam green front hall wall and announce that it was made in the Black Forest and given to her as a wedding gift by her beloved Aunt Edna.

Chas had the idea that he could fix the cuckoo clock. If he could tinker a little with its internal mechanisms, he thought that he could get the cuckoo bird to pop out of its trap door on the hour rather than twelve minutes after the hour. Heavens knows where he came up with this idea. He was just a skinny little seven and a half year old kid who had never fixed anything in his life, but had taken a number of things apart.

Just last week he took apart the waffle iron and, of course, could not put it back together again. His Mom was really annoyed and even his Dad was somewhat perturbed because he liked waffles for breakfast with a lot of butter and maple syrup filling the little square indentations in each waffle. After Chas tinkered with the waffle iron, his Dad had to make do with toast for breakfast. This event resulted in a reduction of Chas' weekly allowance to zero, which did not bother Chas a whole lot because his allowance had already been reduced to zero after some bad behaviour during Sunday services at St. Wilhelmina's church that occurred two weeks prior to the waffle iron incident.

Putting action to his idea, Chas hauled the antique piano stool from its place in front of the Lingoober up-right piano in the living room to right in front of the cuckoo clock in the adjacent front hall. Chas knew that the piano stool was an antique because his Mom had told him so on numerous occasions. The piano stool was not a wedding gift from Aunt Berna or from Aunt Edna, but it was the outcome of a purchase by Chas' parents at Don's Resale Shoppe. This piano companion had a carved wooden base with three fascinating wooden claws at the bottom, each claw clutching a glass ball and each glass ball resting on the floor. Chas had a vague idea that anything purchased at a "Shoppe" had seen better days.

By the way, the piano stool had a fascinating, upholstered, heavily worn, round seat that could spin on its carved wooden shaft. The revolving action of the piano stool seat was probably meant to allow an accomplished pianist, after performing a very difficult piano piece by Chopin, perhaps his Sonata No. 2, to spin around to face an appreciative audience and receive loud and long applause without having to bother to stand up. Whatever the reason for a spinning top on a piano stool, there now existed an interesting mix of a cuckoo clock on the wall, a piano stool on the floor in front of the clock and a little kid intent on fixing the clock.

There was a strict rule in the Lingoober home that no-one ever, without exception, was permitted to stand on the furniture. Applying this rule to the piano stool, Chas should not ever stand on the stool, which was included as a piece of furniture in the Lingoober home. Chas apparently forgot this rule as he climbed on to the stool and, with his hands on the sea-foam green papered wall for support, slowly stood up. The round top of the piano stool was a little wobbly, probably because the stool was an antique from Don's Resale Shoppe, which was also an appropriate reason why no-one should ever stand on it.

Just as Chas stood up on the wobbly piano stool, the top of the stool with Chas standing on it slowly began to turn. The turning motion may have been caused by Chas pushing against the wall as he slowly stood up.

Whatever the reason, the top of the wobbly stool was now in motion at the exact same moment that Chas stood on his tiptoes while stretching his arms high over his head in order to remove the cuckoo clock from the wall.

What happened next was something like a ballet, a very poorly performed ballet. The top of the stool continued its circular motion and Chas desperately tried to maintain his balance on the wobbly seat while holding the clock above his head. He was miserably unsuccessful in maintaining his balance. In fact, Chas lost his balance with his skinny right leg going into the air like a not too graceful ballet dancer as he slowly fell backwards, with a look of enormous surprise on his face and a scream stifled in this throat.

The cuckoo clock, the one that was the wedding gift from his Mom's beloved Aunt Edna, went flying through the air. It flew by itself because Chas spread his arms to try to preserve his balance on the darn revolving wobbly stool, thereby releasing his hold on the clock while at the same time giving it the needed momentum to fly through the air by itself. The clock, which was not constructed for flying, first hit the double doorway located between the front hall and the living room causing some of its critical parts to tumble onto the red carpeted floor. Then the clock fell onto the floor of the front hall leaving some more clock parts scattered on the carpet. Finally, the clock with a will and energy of its own, took a bounce into the living room where it broke into very many pieces.

It was like Humpty Dumpty who fell from a wall and cracked into a million bits. The cuckoo bird popped entirely out of its house on an amazingly long curly-type metal spring and gave a last pathetic peep.

At the same time that the cuckoo clock was encountering its fate, Chas was falling backward from the piano stool with his skinny right leg and foot very high in the air and the other foot still somewhat on the wobbly piano stool. Chas fell so far back in fact that he landed on his head. The red carpet did nothing to cushion his fall. Just as everything was going black, Chas heard his Mom's warbling, high pitch scream.

Several seconds after this fateful event, Chas awoke in a...

COLD SWEAT!!

The
GRANDKIDS

randpa Chas could not understand what posessed him to agree to take his jumpy, bounce-about, over-active grandkids to church on that Sunday. Well, actually just his grandsons, Bart and Wilfred, were rather jumpy, bounce-about, and over-active. His granddaughter, Julene, was really quite well behaved, except when she wasn't so well behaved.

His wife, Grandma Maeve (Grandpa was always amazed that Grandma's parents, who claimed to posess some Irish heritage, named her Maeve, which means "intoxicating" in the Irish tongue) had a way with kids, but was sick with the flu or some other malady or just pretending to be sick in order to have a reprieve from the grandkids. His daughter, Sweet Camilla, and her husband, parents of those kids, were off on a fling in Bermuda.

So, Grandpa was stuck that Sunday with Bart, sometimes called "Barty", who was one year old or maybe two years old or somewhere in between, Wilfred, sometimes called "Willy", who was five years old or maybe six, and Julene who had an age somewhat more than Bart and somewhat less than Willy. Grandma knew how old each kid was and even the date of their births. She also knew the birthdates of Grandpa's numerous siblings and untold number of nieces and nephews. The Church was completely packed with Christians of various statures, sizes and shapes, each decked out in go-to-church finery.

Grandpa and the kids squeezed into a pew at the back of the church. Directly in front of them was a rather large Christian lady and an extra-ordinarily large, one might even say in an un-Christian manner "fat", Christian gentleman. The large lady had an appropriately large head with an enormous amount of reddish hair covered by a truly huge hat, complemented by a full-length what might be mink fur coat. That hat had a remarkably close resemblance to, and may have been a center-piece for a very elaborate dining room table – what with all the fruit and flowers and greens and ribbons included in its make-up. It even had a few feathers and a sprig of holly stuck artfully in its mid-section.

It was difficult to keep one's eyes off that out-size hat, so fascinating and interesting it was, particularly for Bart, who was a perpetual motion gear in Granpa's arms and who continuously stretched his chubby little arms and fingers toward the hat. Grandpa had to really struggle to hold those chubby grabbers away from the Christian lady's head-apparel.

Little Julene, decked out in her go-to-church fancy dress, the red velvety one with pink ribbons, was not causing any bother, but was also not focusing on the religious ceremony. She was reaching across the pew in front of her and slyly stroking the large lady's fur coat and probably thinking how nice it would be if Grandpa would buy her a pet panda bear or perhaps a small chimpanzee with fur like the lady wore.

When Bart was restrained forcibly from doing damage to the hat, he would turn around and focus his wicked attention on Grandpa Chas' face and, in particular, his nose which Bart would grab with his chubby little fingers and yank and twist, all the while laughing as though nose-pulling were the funniest thing in the world. Obviously, Barty had not been taught that nose-pulling was forbidden in church.

Grandpa turned his attention for a moment to Wilfred who shortly before had been leaning on the back of the pew in front of him and looking very bored with the experience. Due to the presence of the large folks in front of them, neither Grandpa nor any of the grand-kids could see the altar or the going-ons at the front of the church. But now, Wilfred was nowhere to be seen! Willy had disappeared. Where the heck was the kid? Just then Grandpa saw him begin to emerge from UNDER the pew with something in his hand that looked like age-old chewing gum.

At that same moment exactly, the large Christian lady in the pew in front of them emitted a deep-throated groan which crescendoed into a full-throated mezzo-soprano-like scream and placed her fleshy hands on her large head WHICH WAS MOSTLY SHINEY BALD due to the horrifying fact that Bart had reached out with his chubby hands attached to his chubby paws and snatched the hat from the lady's

head – the massive amounts of reddish wig hair that were attached to the hat – and stuck a bunch of berry-type hat decorations in his mouth.

The adjacent very large man, who now appeared to be eight feet tall with a corresponding weight, was beginning to turn his large face around to the source of this catastrophe.

JUST THEN, GRANDPA CHAS AWOKE IN A COLD SWEAT!

GROUCHES

My son tonight says life is a bore, Carrying out garbage, a rotten chore..

Attending school is such a bore, At his family he's ticked off and sore.

My daughters argue with such force, They absolutely must have a horse.

They would take care
of it, of course,
For happiness, the
only source.

The wife complains
in a big huff,
I'm not around here
quite enough.

The kids goof off
and all that stuff,
She'd like to kick
them in the duff.

Even grandma seems
nuts these days,
Still claims grandpa
fools around and plays.

Grandpa as usual
feigns a daze,
Doesn't let her
harping at all faze.

My ancient aunt so
conservative, Suddenly
talks silly and glibe.

Apparently wants her
life twice to live,
Wears chains and studs
and carries a shive.

Even the mongrel,
Ozone, urks,
In the bushes she
growls and lurks.

Basic canine duty she
shirks, It acquired the
worst human quirks.

Back to my son, look
at his clothes,
That same black T-shirt
with him grows.

Our suggestions,
he only loathes.
At dressy duds, turns
up his nose.

Perhaps I just don't
understand, but too much
seems wrong in this land.

Those yuppie goals are
made of sand,
by an imaginery hand.

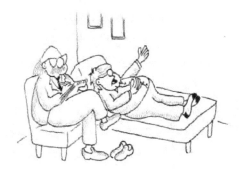

Things we have in
such profusion,
In our minds create
confusion.

Life around us, an illusion,
We suffer mental
contusion.

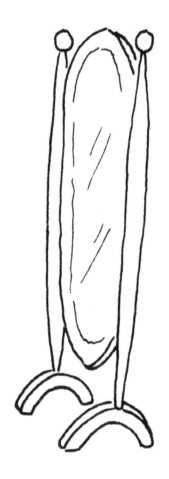

BUDDHA'S

is Mom had given him exactly $3.75 and very exact instructions as to what to do with the cash. Chas was to take his bike (a metallic red Schwinn with fat tires and a big horn that produced an unbelievable amount of noise when Chas squeezed its rubber bulb horn blower) and ride down to Buddha's butcher shop. Once there he was to purchase two pounds of Buddha's finest breakfast sausage and immediately report back home with sausage in hand. There was to be none of the usual dawdling along the way.

The Buddha butcher shop, a somewhat worse for wear one storey building with a large not too clean display window and a creaky paint-chipped door on the front side, was located on Monroe Avenue about a mile from Chas' home on Van Goober Street, in the shadow of the imposing Roman Catholic Cathedral. Shabby Buddha's was the nearest neighbor of the cathedral and for kids and some grown-ups alike, the place of greater interest.

It (Buddha's, not the Cathedral) had a reputation for producing the best sausages in town. Aside from meats and sausages of various interesting and sometimes bloody types, shapes and kinds, there was an assortment of jaw breakers, metal clicker frogs, cigarette lighters and a whole bunch of miscellaneous merchandise of enormous interest to eleven and a half year old Chas Lingoober.

Of greater fascination than the clicker frogs was Buddha himself. A large man with a bald head and droopy mustache, Chas could not stop staring at Buddha's nose hairs and ear hairs, with which the butcher was exuberantly endowed, and the hairs on the back of Buddha's large butcher hands. Chas looked at the back of his hands and wondered if one day his hands would also be furry like Buddha's and tried to see his reflection in the not so clean glass of the not so clean meat showcase to determine it there were hairs coming out of his ears and nose.

"Hey buddy! What can I do for you?"

Buddha's largeness seemed to increase as he said this and his abundant nose hairs dominated his entire head. Chas totally forgot how much sausage he was to purchase pursuant to his Mom's strict instructions. Was it three pounds? No, maybe four pounds! Lacking exact knowledge of how many pounds were required, Chas replied that he wanted this much breakfast sausage and held the palms of his hairless hands about 14 inches apart.

"Ah! You want two pounds of my best sausage. Right, kid? That will be $200!"

Chas' face showed eleven year old type disbelief and shock and turned deep red on hearing the price. The two stared at each other for a moment.

Chas totally uneasy about the price and Buddha with the slightest of grins on his mustached face.

Then Buddha broke into a huge laugh which featured silver encrusted front teeth under the droopy mustache and abundant nose hairs and said that he would sell two pounds of his finest breakfast sausage for $3.50 whereupon the butcher reached into the showcase and grabbed a chunk of sausage that had been displayed there all curled into itself, wrapped it in newspaper and placed it on the counter.

Chas placed a handful of money on the counter from which Buddha took the purchase price at which point the transaction was completed. Chas, now only partially recovered from his price shock, was delighted to note that he still had 25 cents to put back in his pocket.

Taking a last look at Buddha's nose and ears and the clicker frogs, Chas left Buddha's butcher shop with the breakfast sausage, climbed on his metallic red Schwinn bike and started pedaling home, the sausage held in his left hand.

About four blocks up Monroe Avenue from the meat shop, there was another really, really interesting place of business. It was Lehn's Ice Cream Shop! Chas could not resist the temptation to stop in to do some ice cream cone business. Also, it would be a good way to calm his nerves after the Buddha's price shock even though he had been advised by his Mom, in no uncertain terms, that he was to get back to the Lingoober homestead without delay.

The 25 cents in his pocket and the Lehn's ice cream would be a cool combination.

Which indeed it was! Chas was in the forbidden shop with his 25 cents and out in less than four minutes with sausage in one hand and a cherry-delight ice cream cone in the other. He mounted his bike again to get underway, which was not so easy with only two hairless hands. The solution was to steer the Schwinn with his right hand, place the sausage on his head, and keep the left hand free to move the ice cream cone to his face for the purpose of eagerly licking the forbidden 25 cent cherry-delight.

It was only after a few unsteady turns of the pedals of the Schwinn bike when it happened! In seconds, the fat tire of Chas' metallic red Schwinn bicycle hit a half-open man-hole cover causing the sausage to go flying into the middle of Monroe Avenue on the left side. The cherry-delight ice cream cone went flying onto the curb on the right side. Chas went flying straight forward over the handle bars and, horror of horrors, a very large Packard automobile ran over the sausage package with its very large front tire causing the sausage to splat its gut-like contents out of its newspaper package of which a significant amount landed in Chas' hairless face!

JUST THEN, GRANDPA CHAS AWOKE IN A COLD SWEAT!

The CONFOUNDED CHRISTMAS TREE

Grandpa Chas had already picked out what he thought was the perfect Christmas tree and shelled out the exorbitant price of $80 for the privilege of loading it on his GMC SUV and taking it home. (Actually, the SUV belonged to his wife, Mauve, who let him drive it from time to time).

The tree was perfect until Mauve pointed out with a know-it-all air of superiority that the trunk of the tree was crooked, the needles were dry and falling off and one side of the tree looked goofy. Besides, Chas should have purchased a spruce rather than a pine tree.

Muttering that Mauve should pick out the tree herself, if she knew so darn much about the subject matter, Grandpa Chas made his way back to Mo's roadside Christmas tree place and picked out another specimen for the kingly price of $75.99, this time a spruce, from the dwindling supply of the season's most popular evergreen. To avoid his wife calling him a "fruit cake", Chas kept his frequent mutterings to himself.

The thing with the tree was just one reason why Grandpa wished Christmas would be postponed – permanently, at least the part dealing with the tree. Getting a six foot plus tree into the house was a real battle. No type of tree, much less a large Christmas tree, belonged in a house.

It seemed unnatural to Grandpa Chas to have to haul the super big, actually gigantic, tree into the house, to struggle to get it through the doorways which never are wide enough for the perversely unfolding bottom branches, to squeeze it around corners leaving scratches on the walls as evidence of the unfair struggle, and to stuff the tree trunk into a stand. Science and technology has not yet come up with a Christmas tree stand that an ordinary human being of mid-size intelligence, that is, like Grandpa Chas, could handle. It was only with a huge amount of perspiration and some, but not too much (on account of Maeve) inappropriate language, that these chores were accomplished.

But picking out the Christmas tree, too often of imperfect character; sweating to haul it into the house and around corners; and struggling to place it up-right in the stand, were only skirmishes. The real battles were yet to come. Take the lights! Grandpa always wanted to put on the tree a chain of light bulbs, actually many such chains connected to each other, that were large and multi-colored, blue, red, pink, yellow and very expressive, in Grandpa Chas' mind, of the Christmas spirit, which he unfortunately at that moment did not have. If the large colored lights would blink in a random matter, so much the better. However, Maeve would have nothing to do with large colored lights, even though she also had nothing to do with putting the lights on the tree.

Maeve expressed her firm never-to-be questioned opinion that the fat lights belonged only in the local corner tavern.

On the matter of Christmas tree lights, Grandpa Chas annually and bravely took a very hard position but, of course, lost the argument. Every year for twenty years or more, dinky white lights would, and did, go on the family Christmas, Amen!

It was also Grandpa Chas' obligation, imposed on him in no uncertain terms by Mauve, to trim the tree. Actually, Chas did not mind this task, because unlike hauling in and putting up the tree and doing the lights, the Christmas tree decorations did not result in a struggle or much sweat. The family had assembled a wild collection of Christmas tree ornaments and decorations of every imaginable size, color and shape. There was no possible way to mix and match these things because they were simply unmixable and unmatchable.

Every year during the past several decades, Grandpa Chas thought that the perfect Christmas gift for Maeve was one or more new Christmas tree ornaments.

No matter how much she rolled her eys upon receipt of this "perfect" gift, and no matter how often Granpa Chas' kids scolded him for once again choosing a dumb Christmas tree decoration as a gift for their Mom,

Chas could not resist picking up another such gift, typically at a drastically reduced price only available on the day before Christmas when he finally got in the spirit and went on a frantic shopping spree for perfect gifts for his family.

It took Grandpa Chas about four hours, with appropriate breaks for a beer or two, to trim the tree, that is, to load it up with the wild collection of ornaments. The longer the task took with its many beer breaks, the more beautiful the Christmas tree looked to Chas. When finished, the fully decorated tree had a certain fascination, because it was so unusual. Anyone looking at it could not but help think, what the heck went wrong here!

Actually the grandkids, Willy, Julene, Bart and a very recent addition named little Chas, were not very critical of Grandpa Chas' over-decorated Christmas tree. They arrived at Grandpa and Grandma's house on Christmas Day afternoon in wild anticipation of a load of presents.

Grandma Maeve never disappointed them. The grandkids feasted on toys called "Hank the Train", or something like that, "Marble Works, "Hello Kittens", "Your Little Pony" as well as small tools and signature sports clothes for Willy, dragons and pirates for Bart, and princess clothes and hair ribbons for Julene. Grandpa was not sure what kind of presents Little Chas received, perhaps some throw away diapers.

To add to the festive atmosphere, Grandpa put on the CD player the "I Just Go Nuts at Christmas" song, you know, the one sung by the guy with the heavy Swedish accent about the man who, on that jolly holiday, goes into the red like a knock on the head. Grandpa Chas started to gyrate a little to the music, at first doing what looked somewhat like a two-step, then moving to multiple steps while at the same time sashaying his hips.

The song went on in a goofy manner to recount how the man ran into a store on the day before Christmas to buy a nightgown for his wife, but because he did not know her size, he purchased a carpet sweeper for her instead. Grandpa's dancing increased in complexity, if not in style or elegance. He started to pump his arms, shake his head and wave his hands like a traffic cop at a busy corner in Hong Kong.

The grandkids joined in the dancing fun. In particular, Willy went wild, running in circles while slapping his back-side as though he were both horse and rider. Lady-like Julene did not join in the amusement, preferring instead to comb her hair for the twentieth time. But Bart, not to be outdone by his older brother Willy, really went nuts. The "Just Go Nuts at Christmas" song was at the point where someone was saying Merry Christmas and good will to men when just then, in the song, of course, someone slugged Uncle Ben.

It was at that very moment that Bart, wound up like a spinning dervish, grabbed the chain of little twinky lights on Grandpa's Christmas tree and put them around his head like a fiddly-yiddly jerk – those darn lights that were attached to so many other lights on the tree that were attached to the tree itself, causing the Christmas tree accompanied by crescending gasps from all folks of good will present to very slowly, ever so slowly, topple over.

JUST THEN, GRANDPA CHAS AWOKE IN A COLD SWEAT!

HARRY GROSSFIT

Harry Grossfit was so large,
He seemed a hopeless case.

His physique was
like a barge,
A pumpkin was his face.

Enough of looking like a
tub, Of snickers behind
his back, Enough of these
rolls of blub, Of feeling
like a cholesterol sack.

A diet strict would
be the cure,
To Harry's fatty sickness,
To rid him, he felt sure,
Of this unwanted
thickness.

No more ice cream
by the pail,
Away with cookies,
cake, and cream,
He'd eat salad without fail,
And of chocolates
only dream.

The keyword would
be self-denial,
Hot fudge sundaes
he would spurn.
Meals without sweets
might be a trial,
But abstinence he
would learn.

To keep his diet
cholesterol free,
At first was not so hard.
For breakfast melon,
wheatgerm, tea,
At lunch cottage
cheese on chard.

There was more of the
same at dinner,
Lots of lettuce, a little fish.
But, of fine sauces,
not a glimmer,
Nor of any favorite
sweet-tooth dish.

The diet worked,
Harry lost weight,
From quadruple to triple chin.
His dimensions did abate,
He seemed relatively thin.

But his nature once so cheery,
By this diet sorely
tested, Gradually grew
mournful, weary,
Ill-at-ease, and unrested.

For a fancy meal
he did pine,
In violation of his diet.
Once more as a
gourmand to dine,
Why shouldn't he
just try it.

In a four starred
resturant in Atlanta,
On Peachtree Road across
from Lennox Square,
With a chef named
Jean Pierre Ladida,
Harry Grossfit found
the desired fare.

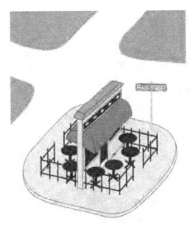

For duck liver as hors
d'oeuvre he didn't care,
But commenced with
oysters on the half shell,
Followed by almond
baked brie with pear,
Snails in garlic butter
and shrimp cocktail.

Cauliflower soup with
lobster and peas,
Was the next course toward
which he felt driven,
Followed by spinach salad
with goat cheese,
Such indulgence should
have been forbidden.

Harry beckoned for
his sommelier,
To order a red wine
of Bordeaux,
Begin with vintage
Domaine de Chevalier,
Thereafter a Premier
Cru Margaux.

Grossfit's hunger
had not abated,
Enormous was his appetite,
His lust for food would
not be sated,
It seemed to grow
with every bite.

Sight of the main course
made his pulse rate climb,
Irregularly throbbed his heart.
Four waiters served the
rack of lamb with thyme,
Mint sauce and
trimmings on a cart.

The shirt he wore seemed
then too tight,
And caused his eyes
somewhat to bulge.
A pain in his side gave
him a small fright,
But stopped not his
need to indulge.

And indulge he did
to the very last,
Consuming all piled on his plate.
Refer to him now as
one in the past,
Since at that meal
he met his fate.

Harry Grossfit expired
that very night,
With his head in chocolate pie,
And on his face a look
of great delight,
So, to Harry and diet,
"Good bye".

Exactly two seconds after he expired, Harry awoke in a cold sweat!!

PROFESSOR CLEM
and
The Big Speech

Professor Clem Hupfenstock wasn't really ready for the key-note speech that he had been asked to present to the members of the local Buffalo Club. The Club was the center, so to speak, of the social and cultural life of the little college town located in the foothills of the Appalachian Mountains.

Clem should probably have considered it an honor to be the focus of attention, even if his selection most probably had been occasioned by the vacation of his colleague, Professor Wittelsdinger, who would surely have been selected as the speaker rather than Professor Clem.

Actually, Professor Clem was not a full professor – his real title was "Adjunct Professor of Business Ethics and Responsibility". It was a position that did not pay very much and did not give Clem much opportunity to come into contact with elite students – for that matter, he was not certain that any elite students attended the College.

During his lectures, the typical student demeanor was one of overwhelming boredom even though Professor Clem tried to enliven his lectures with examples of outrageous Ponzi Schemes, bold embezzlements, fradulent advertisements and other corporate misconduct.

It did not occur to Professor Clem that the lack of student interest might be due to his rhetorically awkward and colorless presentation of the material, or maybe, it was his twenty-two year-old wardrobe.

Clem still wore the suit that he had acquired in college (the same college where he was now employed) with money given to him by his dear Aunt Belinda. That one good suit was dark blue with wide stripes and with pants that had taken on an age-induced shine. It was quite the suit in its day and was worn often when courting his present wife, Hilda.

It did not help that Professor Clem had acquired some significant weight during the past decade and had gone quite bald. His waist circumference was challenging his height, which was an untowering 5'7". This girth growth required the waist and seam of his old suit pants to be expanded from time to time to the point where it was questionable what was holding the pants together. Professor Clem had a faint resemblance to a short, mostly bald and stout but very funny and talented movie star; but Clem was neither funny nor talented, just bald and, to put it kindly, quite corpulent. Professor Clem had serious financial problems. Just two days ago, he received a letter from the Sunrise Trust & Loan Bank, the local Bank that was situated in a building fashionable in the early 1920's and that held the mortgage on the bungalow that he and Hilda purchased two years ago. The contents of the letter were shocking – the Bank threatened to commence foreclosure proceedings if Clem did not pay all past-due amounts of principal and interest within thirty days.

Corporate Misconduct Formula

$$A+B=\frac{C-AB}{2} \times \frac{1}{A}(C+B)$$

$$\frac{(W+\underline{H})}{2} \times 0 = (C-A) + \frac{(R-\underline{E}+S)}{5}$$

$$T(H)+I=\frac{S \times I(S)}{2} - S+T+U(\frac{P-\underline{I}+\underline{D}}{2})$$

$$C\frac{(L+\underline{E})}{4} - M = I + S\frac{(\underline{A})}{2}D + \frac{(U-\underline{M})}{2} + (M-Y)$$

The root cause for the disturbing letter from the Bank was that no payments had been made on the bungalow mortgage for several months due to a current liquidity deficit experienced by the Hupfenstocks. This crisis was caused by a stupid investment Professor Clem had made in Goldbotics Inc., a start-up company.

Goldbiotics had promised with a great deal of fanfare to develop and commercialize break-through, revolutionary technology that would facilitate the discovery of oil and gold. This wonder was to be made possible by a machine placed in an aircraft that flew over mountainous topography not easy to reach by land routes. The machine could scan the terrain and reveal where the gold and oil deposits were located. Unfortunately, the technology was a flop. It only worked in fairy story books.

Professor Clem had overlooked telling Hilda about the investment with the result that she wasn't speaking to him much now. She called him a fruitcake. The mortgage money had been used for that unhappy investment.

"Goverment Policy And Corporate Ethical Misconduct: A way out of the Morass" was the ambitious title of his speech. Professor Clem had serious trouble focusing on the preparation of the big speech. His mind, indeed his whole being, was overwhelmed by the Bank's threat to foreclose on his bungalow. He wished he could find a way out of the morass, but that did not seem likely in the near future.

The Buffalo Club was a big deal. Like many towns in the area, his college town had established a club named after a large animal. The Buffalo membership included all the local bigwigs: Honorable George Smidge, Chief Judge of the Circuit Court; Reverend Karl Benedictus, Pastor of Saint Wilhelmina Church; Dr. Peter Zahn, the sole dentist in town; Chuck Sharkey, Esq., the senior partner of the two man law firm, Getum and Sharkey; Heinrich Leib, the local undertaker; and Mayor Chas Lingoober. In all, the club had twenty-two members, each member an exceptionally important person in his own right, or at least in his own mind. Of course, no women were allowed in the club. The ladies were active in the Church Auxiliary.

On the day of the speech, Professor Clem was not feeling well at all. His asthma was acting up again and it seemed that he had a touch of gout or some other large man's ailment which caused persistent pain in his large legs. His wife, Hilda, was still not talking much with him due to the investment gone bad and the problems with the Sunshine Bank. Clem was still a fruitcake in Hilda's mind.

The professor had to make his own breakfast of a hard roll, marmalade which had an odor as though it was on the verge of going bad, and coffee. He reviewed his speech notes at the kitchen table and scribbled some improvements in the margin.

He tried to think of a joke that might be inserted in the speech, but was hopelesly unsucessful in that effort. His mind was preoccupied with the Sunshine Bank letter, which he read again during breakfast.

The Professor stuffed the notes in the pocket of the coat of his old dark blue striped suit, the one with the shiny pants and headed to Glosky's Ballroom where the Buffalo Club held their monthly meetings. Actually, the Ballroom did not resemble in the least any forum where a ball or any fine event would be held. It was the somewhat dingy and worse-for-wear back room of Glosky's Tavern on MainStreet, one block east of the 1920's building housing the Sunshine Trust and Loan Bank.

Professor Clem arrived at the Ballroom just as the President of the Buffalo Club, the owner of the local car dealership, was opening the meeting. Professor Clem ambled to the stage on which a speaker's stand awaited him. As he approached the stage, Clem pulled the papers out of his his pocket to take a last look at his notes. He was shocked to discover that what were in his hand were not his notes at all, but rather that nasty multi-page letter from the Sunshine Trust & Loan Bank.

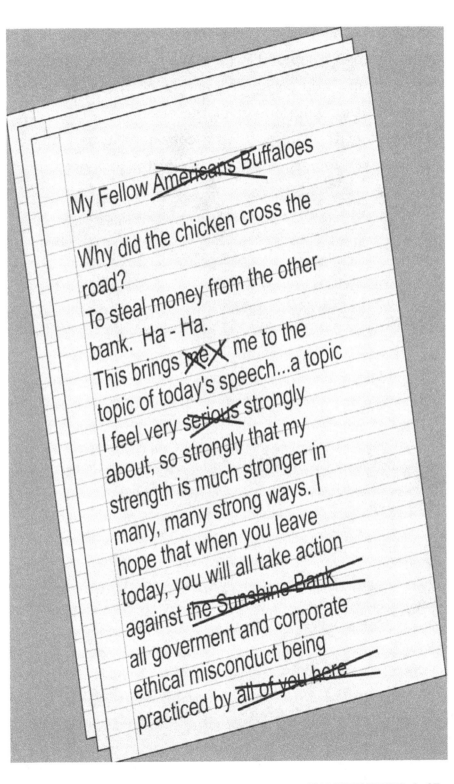

At the same moment, the physical action of raising his bulky right leg to step up on to the stage caused his tired, old pants seam to rip completely and loudly revealing to the open-mouthed amazement of the assembled, honorable members of the Buffalo Club a considerable part of the backside of Professor Clem's polka-dotted underwear.

JUST THEN, PROFESSOR CLEM HUPFENSTOCK AWOKE IN A COLD SWEAT!

The WEDDING

Chas Lingoober was a lonely man. No-one, but no-one, was paying any attention to him. His daughter, Bea, was going to be married in August and Chas had made a number of excellent suggestions regarding details of the wedding, none of which had been accepted, much less implemented. In fact, his wife, Maeve, who was in total command of the Lingoober household, everyone in it, and it seemed, anyone who came into contact with it, and much of what was outside the household, dismissed his excellent ideas in cool disdain and stated in no uncertain terms that they must have come from a "fruitcake".

One of his better suggestions was to hand out a box-lunch to each attendee at the wedding service as he or she came out of Saint Wilhelmina's, affectionately known to the locals as "Mina's", the local church where the wedding ceremony was to take place. Chas was certain that the guests would be delighted to stand around outside of the church, getting to know one-another while munching on a hot-dog (or other morsel of that variety) and a piece of cake and washing it down with a carbonated drink served up in a small plastic bottle with a festive ribbon.

Chas knew the owner of the local gas-station who claimed to be talented at making sushi and who would be willing to supply some of this gourmet item for inclusion in the box-lunch. Or perhaps something organic could be included – like a carrot or a slice of rutabaga.

A particular benefit of this type of celebration would be avoiding the need to rent a hall or other premise for a wedding reception, thereby keeping the costs to a minimum. This idea was met with looks from the women folk in his family and from the many women friends of such women folk indicating that he must have lost his wits.

Chas also tried to persuade his to-be-married daughter, Bea, to purchase or rent a "certified pre-owned" wedding dress, rather than fork out thousands of dollars for a new one. It was his (as usual faulty) understanding that such dresses were available through various charitable organizations or consignment "shoppes" (understanding that a "shoppe" was a very high-class "shop") located in the Appalachian mountain area where the Lingoober family lived. He thought it was possible to obtain a "dress fax" which described the primary characteristics of the prior dress owner and other important, interesting and sometimes intimate information. Bea was shocked and mortified that her father made this suggestion and punished him for it by not talking to him for a full two weeks.

One idea that Chas Lingoober felt certain would receive enthusiastic reception from the many women in his family was Chas himself providing the entertainment at the wedding reception. Mauve had decided that Bea's wedding reception would be held in a hall somewhere in the area, in any event not on the church steps.

The "ballroom" next to the Buffalo Club headquarters came to mind, although that facility was somewhat worn and very much in need of a fresh paint job.

Chas' idea was that he would be the sole music provider at no cost to anyone. He could play the piano (somewhat) and could sing (loudly and only somewhat off-key) and thereby surely keep the wedding guests somewhat entertained and amused. He had in mind mimicking that Swedish guy, Victor Borga, (or was he Norwegian?) who (unlike Chas) played the piano quite well, was quite funny and had quite a knack of causing his grand-piano to collapse in the middle of a number. Chas thought about putting together a medley of songs as the center piece of his performance. Actually, any medley would only consist of the few lines he actually knew of songs like: "Build Me Up Buttercup", "Friends in Low Places", "Wooly Bully", "Easy to Love" and "You'll Never Walk Alone", with perhaps a refrain or two from "People Will Say We're In Love" or from "Coro Di Schiavi Ebrei" as an encore.

In reflecting on the show that he would perform at Bea's wedding reception, Chas could almost hear the thrilling crescendo of shouts for endless encores from the crowd of enthusiastic wedding guests. Just thinking in advance about his super successful performance put a big smile on Chas' face and gave him a feeling of immense satisfaction and well-being. This well-being thing was deflated totally and mercilessly by Mauve when he dared to mentioned this brilliant entertainment (and cost saving) idea to her one night at the dinner table.

Mauve suggested that he should limit his musical exercises to the bathroom. Chas muttered something unkind and possibly unprintable, which is why what he muttered is not repeated here.

On the day prior to the big event, Chas was ordered by Mauve to drive into town for the purpose of picking up Bea's brand new (not certified pre-owned) and very fancy wedding dress and at the same time taking receipt of a tuxedo and formal footwear required for the march with his daughter down St. Mina's Church aisle. He set off in his smallish, no longer newish, foreign-made automobile for the drive to the town center. The weather was not very good, although there were promises of sunshine and warm temperatures for the wedding day tomorrow. Right now, however, it was pouring puddle-creating rain.

He drove to the main street of North Bucklore, which appropriately enough was called "Main Street" and looked for a parking place. The fancy wedding dress place and the tuxedo store were only a block apart and across from the County Courthouse, but on the same side of Main Street as Pete's Bikers Bar. The Bar's clever motto was: "Better In Here Than Across The Street In The Courthouse", although from time to time a Biker Bar's patron appeared as a defendant in the Courthouse in a petty burglary, assault, forgery or other criminal case.Chas luckily found a parking spot between two super large motorcycles in front of the Bar.

Perhaps influenced by the lousy weather, he was at first tempted to go in and have a very small beer prior to undertaking his Mauve-dictated chores.He successfully rejected that evil temptation.

Despite such initial success he found himself nonetheless in Pete's place with a large beer in front of him, there of course being no such thing as a small beer in that establishment. Chas felt like a tough guy in the Bikers Bar where the folks who hung out there generally were of beefy stature, wore beat-up leather outfits, had rings in their ears and noses, among other places, and felt no compelling obligation to either bathe or comb their hair.

And, their hogs, that is, their two-wheeled conveyance vehicles known to common people as motorcycles, were neatly parked in front of Pete's Bikers Bar directly on Main Street and directly across from the imposing Courthouse, which in its court-yard there was featured a statue of a local civil war veteran mounted on a horse. The guy next to Chas at the bar looked like he came directly from Central Casting – tall and thin, in full, well-worn, biker regalia including a lot of Harley-Davidson and gang patches, with a bandana around his head, a longish nose, Rasputin-type greenish-brown eyes peering through metal-rimmed glasses and a skinny unshaven face, scarred from gang warfare and a dissipate life. He could have stumbled out of one of those new-age movies featuring a gang of ruffians in a post-apocalypse setting who attempt to save what is left of the world from two-headed aliens. He called himself "Rembrandt".

For the next two hours and eighteen minutes, Rembrandt gave Chas a recital of his life, or most of it, including his jail time and his current mission to save the world since Rembrandt had recently embraced radical evangelical born-again religion. It was apparent that he thought Chas needed redemption. Chas wasn't so sure about Rembrandt's redemption variety because he was having a hard enough time with Mauve's mandatory redemption lectures. Nonetheless Chas gifted Rembrandt several beers as a gesture of good will.

When Rembrandt eventually stumbled off to the restroom, Chas glanced at his watch and was shocked to discover that the wedding dress and tuxedo places would close in less than fifteen minutes. He hurriedly paid for his two beers and Rembrandt's four beers and rushed out of the Biker Bar, turned left and found his way to Shirley's Wedding Apparel, exactly where it was supposed to be at 729 Main Street as set forth on Mauve's instructions.

The proprietress, Shirley herself, a woman of multiple divorces and of imposing proportions, a slight mustache and, even for such a small town, archly overbearing manners, was annoyed that Chas Lingoober showed up so late in the day to claim his daughter's dress. Shirley gave him a long-winded and condescending speech about care of the dress, as though Chas was the person who would be caring for it, none of which Chas comprehended, her words going in one ear and out the other.

Chas grabbed the dress without paying particular attention to its excessive length and multiple folds, that is, he did not treat it very delicately, and made his exit back onto Main Street. There he turned left and several stores down entered Rocky's Tuxedo Emporium which was correctly located at 735 Main Street, exactly where Mauve said it would be.

The proprietor, Rocky himself, a balding bachelor of diminutive stature who sported a slight mustache, handed Chas a box containing shiny formal shoes and a garment bag enclosing the tuxedo and accessories. Rocky suggested that Chas try on the shoes and tuxedo to make certain they fit properly, but Chas declined thinking that he had better rush home to avoid a severe scolding from his wife, Mauve, for not showing up two hours ago with wedding dress in hand.

About a half hour later, Chas triumphantly entered the Lingoober home and carefully placed the wedding dress across the kitchen table for all to see. Unfortunatelyfor Chas, he did not see the slice of one-hundred per cent whole wheat, fiber-filled, no high fructose bread on the table smeared with what appeared to be a pound of sticky peanut butter and wiggly jelly, courtesy of his grandson, Willy. The dress was placed square across the Willy's peanut butter and jelly open-faced sandwich, which caused Mauve to let out a blood-curdling yell, which was joined by loud exclamations and schrieks from his daughters,

Camilla and Bea, and all the other women who then happened to be in the house, and, it seemed to Chas, a whole bunch of folks in the neighborhood, so loud and unsettling was the yelling and goings-on.

To add to this frightful cacophony of noise, each of his grandchildren, starting with Willy and joined by Bart and even by perfectly polite Julene, joined in the screeching just for the fun of it. Little Chas, the youngest grandchild then seated in a high-chair, knocked his bowl of Cheerios on the floor, as his contribution to the confusion. The noise was clearly excessive because, upon inspection, no damage was done to the wedding dress due to its clear plastic wrapping. However, that redeeming circumstance did not help Chas a lot. The women folk glared at him as though the dress had been completely covered by brownish peanut butter and reddish strawberry jam stains and the whole wedding affair had been completely ruined. His grandkids suggested that Grandpa Chas be made to take a time-out (an event each kid experienced several times a day) until he learned to behave.

All the other women in the house included, among others, Betty, Liz, Candy, Franny and Lulu, who claimed to be Chas' sisters and who were there to help meddle in the wedding and to otherwise add their respective two-cents worth of advice. Chas figured their advice combined was worth well less than two cents.

Betty was a whole lot older than Chas and was still resentful because he pushed her off Kelly's Hill in a game of King of the Mountain, thereby claiming permanently and rightfully the King of the Mountain title. That incident occurred about fifty years ago. Actually, Chas did not just push her off: he really sent her flying, that is, air-borne, to a butt-down, hard landing at the bottom of Kelly's Hill to his great delight and to Betty's huge and enduring disbelief.

Liz was still annoyed because Chas caught her smoking unfiltered Camel cigarettes in a closet of their family home on South Coolidge Street. Those nasty cigarettes had been purloined from their Dad. Liz was required to pay Chas twenty-five cents a week for about a year as a gratuity to prevent him from reporting this incident to their parents. That event also occurred a long time ago.

Everyone knew that Candy cut the tops off their neighbor's prize tulips when she was four years old, but only Chas thought it was very funny to keep bringing the matter up at family gatherings.

Franny was not in Chas' good graces because she recently suggested that his garden was full of weeds. Obviously, she could not tell weeds apart from healthy leafy, semi-organic, vegetable plants.

Lulu was upset with Chas because he told her that her favorite professional football team should be disbanded due to incompetence and that the local high school football team could whip the pants off her team. Actually, Chas sort of liked his many sisters, even though they took every occasion to gang up on him. This recessed animosity might also stem from the fact that his sisters did not fare as well as each of them desired in a very successful and widely acclaimed novel published by Chas that purported to be a partially apocryphal Lingoober family biography.

The big day finally arrived. The sun was in full shine, the birds were chirping and the world seemed to be rotating more or less correctly on its axis. Chas Lingoober felt like a big-shot while putting on his tuxedo. Too bad that the mirror revealed that the tux trousers were several sizes too big and the shiny patent-leather shoes were at least one size too small. Darn! He should have tried them on as Rocky, the balding formal-wear guy with the mustache, had suggested. It was too late now! Upon viewing the baggy trousers, Mauve gave him a verbal blast and suggested,once again, that he was a fruitcake. Well under his breath, Chas called her something that rhymed with "itch" and began with a "w". The extra-large, bunched in the front, pants were a small problem, fixed in part by wearing the quite fashionable cummerbund unfashionably and ridiculously low on his waist, which over the years had expanded in a stately manner, but not enough to satisfy the extra-large dimensions of the tux trousers.

The bigger problem were the extra-small shoes, in which Chas shoe-horned his feet, that is, his soon to be severely aching feet.

At the Saint Mina's Church, everything seemed to be going well, until one of the flower-basket kids, namely Chas's grandson, Bart, tried to stick a rose petal in the nose of his sister, Julene, which situation very soon deteriorated into rose and other flower parts being tossed, stomped on and otherwise scattered all over the foyer of the Church. The various statues of the saints that dignified that foyer looked rather gravely on the antics of the flower kids. Particularly Saint Philomena seemed to be concerned with the un-Churchlike conduct. Camilla had her hands full restoring order. Each of her kids involved in the disorder was made to take a time-out in a corner of the Church foyer beneath the statue of a frowning saint.

Chas was not paying much attention to the distractions caused by the flower-basket grand-kids, because he was focusing on the newly discovered realization that he could not move his toes, so tightly and so painfully were they wedged into his fancy rented patent-leather too small shoes.

Then the pipe-organ of St. Wilhelmina swelled in a glorious crescendo with the opening bars of the Bridal Chorus from Wagner's "Lohengrin".

Bea looked positively gorgeous. Chas's pinched feet were killing him. The flower kids were sent on their way down the aisle followed by innumerable bridesmaids and the maid-of-honor. Now it was the big moment for Bea and her father.

The Reverend Karl Benedictus was standing at the front of the Church facing the congregation, as was the groom and each of the best men. The Reverend Benedictus was looking at his watch, probably wondering if the wedding ceremony would be over in time to make his tee-off at the Appalachian Valley Golf Club.

Many of the guests were rubber-necking toward the back of the Church in order to view the bride being escorted down the aisle by Chas. There was the Honorable George Smidge, Chief Judge of the Circuit Court, with his wife, Booty and in the next pew, Chas spied the toothy grin of Dr. Peter Zahn, the sole dentist in town. On the other side of the aisle stood grim-faced Chuck Sharkey, Esq., the senior partner of the two man law firm, Getum and Sharkey. Chuck's wife, Hildegard, was also in attendance as was Henry Leib, the local undertaker, and his deathly-pale wife, Loretta.

Now Chas offered his arm to Bea and the two began the walk down the aisle. Chas's pinched feet hurt so much that tears were rolling out of his eyes. This teary-eyed state of affairs caused a number of the congregation, in a sympathetic reaction to what they mistakenly thought were Chas's tears of joy, to themselves well up with tears.

Chas tried walking on the sides of his feet, which made him look peculiar indeed, something like an emperor penguin. It must have been about half-way down the aisle that it happened, something that never before in the annals of wedding-day history had occurred: Chas stopped the march with Bea to the front of St. Mina's, bent over and took off his way-too-small shoes and then continued on his way in socking feet with a look of huge relief on his face.

JUST THEN, GRANDPA CHAS AWOKE IN A COLD SWEAT!

The WHEELBARROW

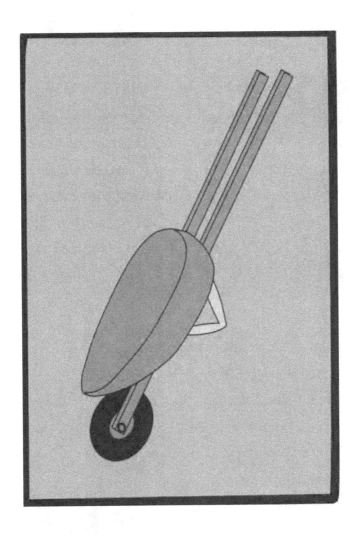

Barrel and wheel, a
wheelbarrow they call,
Trash, junk and stuff
it's intended to haul.
And ripened manure from
the farmer's mound,
In the garden to cart
and spread around.

The barrel was used
for another chore,
Which could be considered
often a bore.
Moving the garbage from
backyard to curb,
There left for garbage
men, Clifton and Merv.

Now it must be told, three
brothers had Clem,
They were not very
clever, no not them.
All were younger, Clem -
smarter and older,
Which somehow made
them goofy and bolder.

The brothers three, nutty
things they tried,
In a wheelbarrow now
they wanted to ride.
Knowing full well that for
human live freight,
The barrow with garbage
hardly did rate.

So then Clem into that
barrow loaded,
Garbage and boys, it
nearly exploded.
The garbage center, the
boys on the side,
Wiggling and squirming
all set for the ride.

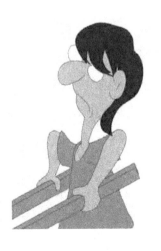

'Cause, though Clem was
smart, he wasn't so strong,
In hindsight he guessed
perhaps it was wrong.
That barrow with boys
weighed nearly a ton,
Clem wasn't sure this could
be so much fun.

Clem grabbed the handles
and got underway,
This was work for him,
for the boys just play.
They laughed and shouted
as it picked up speed,
Too bad later the doctor
they would need.

The driveway was long
and made of cement,
The barrow rattled and
creaked as it went.
Accelerated through
forces unknown,
It seemed to acquire
a will of its own.

The laughter heard evolved
soon into screams,
From three little boys and
Clem too it seems.
By now they were flying,
that much was clear,
The cargo up front and
Clem at the rear.

The driveway inclined
on a downhill grade,
Which made Clem more
than a little afraid.
The barrow began to
yaw and sway,
Tipped left, then tipped
right, it seemed to sashay.

A piercing loud yell just
then did Clem hear,
This very day it
resounds in his ear.
He looked around to
discover its source,
And spied his Mom, he should
have known, of course.

At that split second Clem's
hands lost their grip,
The wheelbarrow was
a rudderless ship.
Ploughing abandoned with
its human live freight,
That ship the boys
tried to evacuate.

The scene was wild, there
was so much noise,
The wheelbarrow pitched
over, so did boys.
With the garbage, in
fact, they went flying,
Found themselves later
on the street lying.

Clem himself tumbled and
into the street rolled,
Flipped on his head and was
nearly knocked cold.
The three youngsters from
bruising fared worse,
Though for none was there
need to call the hearse.

After this episode so
harrowing, Clem then
and there renounced
wheelbarrowing.
Those three bruised
boys went back to their
peashooters,
Their little wagons, trikes
and red scooters.

JUST THEN, CLEM AWOKE IN A COLD SWEAT!

THE END OF THE WORLD!

The end of the world was to occur at four o'clock in the afternoon on August 24. That was the prophecy of Brother Axel Rodenkirk. He was the leader of the Good Saints hermits and their lady friends. They lived at the edge of town in a settlement located near a long-ago closed coal mine. The Good Saints clan was founded in the early 1970's by Brother Axel and a bunch of his flipped-out hippie friends.

It was rumored that the Good Saints smoked marijuana and carried on in ways that in no manner could be called saintly. They all had long stringy grey hair and wore patched trousers and shirts picked up at the local charity warehouse and sandals home-made from rubber tire remnants. The Saints made their living by selling organic vegetables of dubious origin and of dubious organic quality. They also engaged in aggressive panhandling after the service on Sunday morning at St. Wilhelmina's Church.

Brother Axel had proclaimed the end of the world in July, not more than one month ago. He did so while sitting on the bronze horse featured prominently in the center of the lawn in front of the courthouse of the little Appalachian town of North Bucklore. The silent and immobile bronze rider of that bronze horse was also present sitting metallic straight and tall behind the grey bearded Brother Axel. The rider was a lesser known Major who was born in North Bucklore and who had performed some lesser known heroic act during the Civil War.

The courthouse was located on Main Street directly across the street from Pete's Biker Bar. The Bar was well known for the sign in its window proclaiming that it was better to be in the Biker Bar than across the street in the Courthouse.

Professor Clem Hupfenstock, of course, did not believe that the world would come to an end today, which happened to be THE DAY. He thought that Brother Axel was a little goofy, that is, somewhat weak in the head. His wife, Hilda, called Brother Axel a nut and paid him no heed.

Despite this non-belief, Clem was a little nervous and uncertain about what might happen later today. Perhaps if Clem had given the Good Saint panhandlers some loose change after Sunday services, the end of the world would not have been set for this afternoon. But, as already stated, the world was not going to end today or any time soon ... or so Clem tried to convince himself.

Some North Bucklore residents took the end of the world announcement seriously, so seriously, in fact, that a delegation of town citizens met with Brother Axel to find out whether the end of the world could be postponed because many of them still had tasks that could only be accomplished after four p.m. on THE DAY. The undertaker, Heinrich Leib, had organized a funeral next week for the brother of Chief Judge George Smidge.

The person of honor, that is, the deceased guy, was also a cousin of Gus Jeckley, the President of the Buffalo Club. There would be a big wake attended by all the dignitaries of North Bucklore and, of course, all the members of the Buffalo Club and their respective wives. And Gus, who owned the Bucklore Finer Pre-Owned Car Emporium, had planned for some very fine gently used automobiles to be delivered to his showroom located on Main Street not far from the Courthouse and across from Glosky's Tavern, where the Buffalo Club held its meetings. But Brother Axel was absolutely firm that the end of the world could not be postponed. It would occur irrevocably and without delay this afternoon at four o'clock. The funeral and the delivery of fine used cars and everything else that the good citizens of North Bucklore were planning next week and thereafter would have to be cancelled.

During the prior week, the Mayor of North Bucklore, Chas Lingoober, shook hands with other town officials as though he was retiring from office or as though he was being transferred to an official position in the State Capital. The Buffalo Club called an extraordinary meeting of its members for the purpose of celebrating, three months' early, the twelfth anniversary of its founding. Of course, no specific mention was made of the imminent end of the world although the serious facial expressions of certain of the Buffalos suggested that it was on their collective minds.

Father Benedictus told the members of his church to ignore the end of the world announcement, although he did suggest that advantage should be taken without delay of any available indulgences which might save them from difficulties in the afterlife. In the meantime, Father Benedictus scheduled a tee-off time at the local country club for four p.m. today.

On this Saturday morning, as on every Saturday morning, Professor Clem was supposed to scrub the kitchen floor in order to have it clean for Sunday. Hilda insisted that he perform this menial chore even though Clem thoroughly disliked having anything to do with house cleaning. He considered floor scrubbing and all house work as very un-professorial. After all, he was an Adjunct Professor of Business Responsibility and Ethics at the local community college. The result was that the kitchen floor often seemed to be dirtier after Clem did the scrubbing than before.

In order to avoid having to do the floor today, Clem suggested to Hilda that the world was coming to an end this afternoon and therefore it made little sense to scrub the floor. Of course, Clem did not believe what he said about the end of the world, but thought nonetheless that it might be useful as an excuse to avoid having to scrub the floor. Hilda reacted to this suggestion with multiple exaggerated facial and strong verbal expressions of disgust and proclaimed in no uncertain terms that Clem was to scrub the kitchen floor today, and without delay, and the floor had better be mighty clean! Clem mumbled under his breathe something unprintable.

Clem wandered around the house for a while. Something was on his mind. Although he did not at all believe that the world would come to an end later that day, he felt a little uncomfortable because it was a long time that he had done any good deed. Actually he could not remember when the last time was when he performed a good deed. He look around for a good deed, that is, for the occasion prior to four o'clock to do a good deed, perhaps, a very good deed. In fact, he hoped he could do a such a good deed that it would make up for all the good deeds that he did not perform in his life.

In the living room of the Hupfenstock home, Clem heard the tweeting of his wife's beloved and highly prized parakeets. There were two of them in a wire cage hanging from a hook on the wall. The cage was a bird paradise with ladders for climbing practice, swings for swinging, various types of exotic seeds to satisfy the most demanding parakeet appetite, mirrors to allow the birds to admire themselves, and other devices that only the most spoiled parakeets would desire. One parakeet had blue feathers and the other had yellow feathers. One was named "Tweety" and the other was called "Twinkie". Clem was not sure which bird was Tweety and which was Twinky and never cared much about their existence. Clem thought these were really dumb names. He would had called them "Socrates" and "Aristotle", or perhaps "Max" and "Moritz", but Hilda did not ask for his advice in the naming of her feathered friends.

Hilda was extremely fond of these dumb birds. She would talk with them several times a day. It seemed that Clem's wife actually could speak a parakeet language, judging from the parakeet type sounds she made when she visited their cage.

Professor Clem knew that he had found a good deed, in fact, a very good deed! He took the cage with Tweety on a ladder and Twinkie preening himself in front of the mirror from the hook on the wall over to the living room window. He opened the window. Then he opened the door of the wire cage and set the cage on the window sill with the cage door facing the great outdoors. The birds did not seem to want to leave their palace. Clem ran his finger over the cage wires in a way that caused a scary noise, a least scary for the birds. Tweety and Twinkie hopped over to the cage door. That's when Clem shook the cage causing the two birds to fly out the window, whereupon Clem promptly closed the window.

It was at that point that two events occurred, one somewhat more important that the other: Hilda came into the living room, saw what Clem was up to and let outa scream that was the mother of all screams, past, present and what was left of the future AND immediately following that scream and perhaps caused by it, the world came to an end. It was exactly four o'clock in the afternoon.

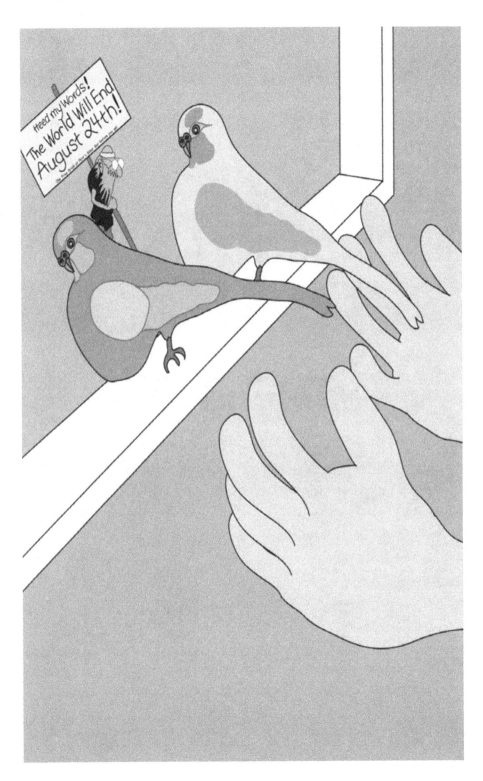

THE END

OTTO and the KETTLE DRUMS

Chas Lingoober was invited by his parents to attend the 1956 season's opening concert of the North Bucklore Symphony Orchestra that evening. Actually, he was not really "invited", he was told that he would attend this momentous event. His Dad said that Chas should be "a vulture for culture". Chas could not figure out the connection between a vulture and the Orchestra although he thought it amusing to picture the Orchestra members as vultures.

He much preferred rock 'n roll to the music produced by the NB Symphony Orchestra. In particular he liked a new song "Love Me Tender" sung by Elvis, The King. Somehow Chas connected the song's romantic lyrics with his hopeless crush on a very pretty, dark eyed girl in his grade school class named Judy, who paid him no attention whatsoever. Having just turned eleven years old, Chas was "feeling his oats" as his Uncle Clarence told Chas's Mom with a weird smirk on his face. Mom told her brother, Clarence, that he had spent way too much time in his youth feeling his oats.

The North Bucklore Symphony Orchestra was made up of volunteers, somewhat like the North Bucklore Volunteer Fire Department.

One time when his cousin, Eddy "accidentally" set on fire a pile of leaves located as a temptation to small time arsonists on the curb of the neighbour's place down the street, the NB VFD really put on a show. Ed claimed that he was just trying

to start a small fire rubbing sticks together like the Indians did hundreds of years ago when they lived and hunted in the area which is now North Bucklore. When he was unsuccessful with the sticks, Eddy got some matches and started a small fire which very soon, actually immediately, swelled into a big fire engulfing the entire leaf pile.

Mrs. Gossum, who lived across the street from the leaf pile and several houses down from the Lingoober home had watched Ed's minor arson from behind the curtain of her living room window. She was the snitch who called the fire department. Apparently she reported that the fire was about to consume her house as well as all the other places on North Howard Street. Old lady Gossum was a person of interest because she dyed her hair purple, wore at least two flashy rings on each finger of her hands and had more wrinkles on her face than a chicken has feathers. Her wealthy husband, Justin Gossum, had died years ago under mysterious circumstances.

Three fire trucks arrived with their sirens howling and their lights flashing and blinking. Then to top it off, a ladder truck showed up on the scene as well as two ambulances. The fire trucks parked every which way on North Howard Street, where this event was taking place, and totally blocked traffic. Each fire fighter was all dressed up like a fireman with boots up to his knees, a long black shiny coat held shut with clasps, a hat with a wide curvy brim and a very serious look on his face.

There were about eighteen firemen on the scene running about hauling hoses which were hooked up to the fire hydrant on the corner. The hydrant was the same one that Bruno, the Lingoober's family dog, used on a daily basis, to do his daily thing. In the meanwhile, the leaf pile fire, which turned out to be not very big after all, burned itself out, much to the disappointment of the eighteen volunteer firemen on the scene and very much to the disappointment of old lady Gossum. Eddy got into a whole lot of trouble as a result of the "accidental" leaf pile fire. Just about everyone at his home and in the neighbourhood lectured him about how bad leaf pile fires were. In addition, and much worse, he could not watch TV for a month and his weekly allowance was reduced from twenty-five to fifteen cents a week.

Like the volunteers of the North Bucklore Volunteer Fire Department, the North Bucklore Symphony Orchestra had volunteer guys and gals who played various musical instruments. Some could toot the flute or the baby flute, called the piccolo. Others knew something about playing the violin or the viola, which was a bigger violin, or the cello, which was a still bigger violin, or the bass fiddle, which Chas regarded as the biggest violin of them all.

Then there was Miss Sinisch who played a tube-like thing called a bassoon. Chas was fascinated by the toots and honks that Miss Sinisch produced with her bassoon.

Pierre Noel, a local school teacher, was a master of the French horn and Fritz Neckarfingel, the over-weight baker's assistant, huffed and puffed on the tuba. The uncle of Chas's grade school friend, Karl Luresch, was in charge of two instruments, the clarinet and the oboe. The oboe could make noises like a love sick stray cat out on the town on a moon-lit night. The most fascinating volunteer member of the North Bucklore Symphony Orchestra was Otto Knaap. Otto manned the drums, specifically the kettle drums. Otto was well known and well liked in North Bucklore. He owned a restaurant and candy store on Main Street which featured Knaap Chocolates. His chocolates were hand-made and really were yummy. When Chas was four years old, while visiting Otto's store with his Mom to buy some candy for Christmas, Chas had reached up to the counter to grab a chocolate and, while doing so, tipped over a tray of about thirty of those hand-made chocolates, with a nut on the top of each one of them. All thirty chocolates landed on the floor, actually in every which direction all over the floor. While scrambling to pick them up, Chas stepped on several of the chocolates, making their sweet innards squirt out all over his shoes and causing the situation to go from bad to worse. Chas caught real heck from his Mom and was made to apologize to Mr. Otto, who graciously patted Chas on the head and said something in Germanabout Chas being a "kleiner knirps". As a young boy in the 1870s, Otto had come to North Bucklore with his family from the Black Forest area in Germany.

Chas knew something about the Black Forest because he had dismantled his Mom's treasured cuckoo clock from that part of the world, the one given to her as a wedding present by her dear Aunt Edna. Unfortunately Chas, who thought that the Black Forest was located in Minnesota, was not able to put the cuckoo clock back together, a fact that his Mom mentioned on a too regular basis. The numerous pieces of the dismantled clock, including a set of chains, weights to be attached to those chains, various springs and gears, the big hand and the little hand, and the cuckoo itself, were kept in a cigar box on the phone table located in the small hallway between the kitchen and the dining room of the Lingoober home, for everyone to see every day.

Otto was nearly ninety years old! He actually looked a lot older. His face was all wrinkly and he had about ten strands of white hair standing straight up on his otherwise quite bald head. Chas's sister, Betty, said that Otto was Methuselah, a really, really old gentlemen featured in the Old Testament. Betty was a lot older than Chas and apparently knew about these things. Otto was allowed to pound the kettle drums way past retirement age, mainly because Otto paid the rent for Glosky's Ballroom where the Orchestra practiced once a week and where the concerts were held. After practice, the Orchestra volunteers would spend time downing a few brews at Glosky's Tavern, located in the same building as the Ballroom.

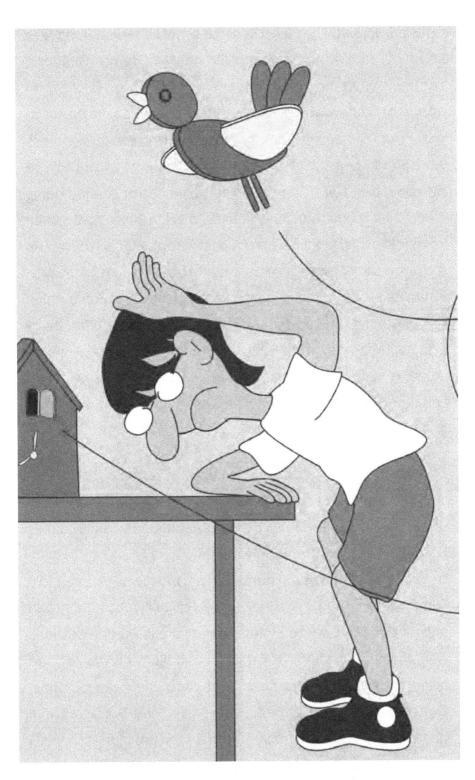

Chas's Dad said that a little more practice and a little less imbibing would increase the Orchestra's fame. Chas did not know what "imbibing" meant, but his sister, Betty, who apparently knew about these things and who was so much older than Chas, said that it meant the Orchestra members were drinking a lot of beer chased by shots of brandy, or maybe it was the other way around, a shot of brandy being chased by a bunch of beers. Even though Chas was eleven years old and thought he knew a lot about a lot of things, he did not understand how a beer could be chased by a brandy. When he pictured in his eleven year old mind several bottles of beer being chased around Glosky's Tavern by a bottle of brandy, he broke into a really loud and quite uncontrollable laugh. It was one of those "ha, ha, ha", "hee, hee, hee" and "huu, huu, huu" laughs that increased in pitch and volume, and inappropriateness, the longer the laugh continued.

This was not at all good because his noisy laughter occurred during Sunday Mass, and specifically during the sermon of Reverend Bede Heilig, the Pastor of Saint Wilhelmina's Catholic Church. The good Reverend was trying to explain the incomprehensible, namely, the mystery of the Holy Trinity, when Chas's untimely laughter interrupted his train of thought. Mr. George Smidge, a very pious Roman Catholic who always put three dollars in the collection basket and who was sitting in the pew immediately in from of Chas, turned around and glared at Chas for the longest time; Chas's sister, Betty, also gave him a "you are in big trouble",

older sister type glare; his Mom pinched Chas's arm to make him stop his laughter and his Dad, after church services were over, said that Chas would receive no allowance for the next six weeks. It seemed that Chas's paltry allowance was always in jeopardy of dissolving into nothing at all.

There was one technical problem with Otto's performance on the kettle drums. Otto could not hear very well and also had some eye defect that made it difficult for him to see Boris Schansky, the Orchestra conductor. The result often was that Otto was still beating the drums after the piece being played had officially come to an end. When that happened, Boris' face would turn a deep red and his wild black curly hair assumed a life of its own, flying around over the top of his head. Boris hinted at social gatherings in North Bucklore that his ancestors were Russian aristocrats. Chas's Dad hinted that Boris came from a family of Serbian coal miners.

At a previous concert of the North Bucklore Orchestra which he was forced by his parents to attend, Chas had been thoroughly amused by the antics of Conductor Shansky's hair after a tardy kettle drum performance by Otto Knaap. He and his friend, Karl, who was also forced to attend the concert, had great fun after-school recreating the scene. Chas would throw his arms every which way and mess up his hair and jump up and down in imitation of Schansky while Karl would beat on an upside-down garbage can, which substituted as a kettle drum, pretending that he was Otto.

Chas as orchestra conductor would attempt to bring Karl's kettle drumming under control while Karl would bang on the garbage can with increasing fury until both of them fell on the ground in a mutual fit of loud and quite outrageous laughter. Chas's sister, Betty, said that it was not very kind to make fun of Otto. Chas told her to go play with her dolls. Karl told her to take a long walk on a short pier, which caused the boys to again break out in ridiculous and exaggerated laughter. The NB Symphony Orchestra was hard at work performing a difficult and quite loud piece by a guy named Mahler. Chas's Mom said Mr. Mahler's first name was "Gustav" and that he was an important composer. Chas wondered if Mr. Gustav Mahler, the composer, was related to Mr. Hank Mahler, the North Bucklore mailman. The music was getting louder. Boris, the conductor, was waving his arms every which way, and it seemed his hips as well, in an effort to maintain, or perhaps regain, control of the Orchestra. The musicians in the string section were sawing away furiously on their violins, cellos, violas and bass fiddles and a couple of horn players actually stood up to play their part, then they sat down again. The oboist, the uncle of Chas' friend, Karl, played his oboe with a rocking motion ... the faster he played, the harder he rocked back and forth. The Mahler music got louder and louder and then, without advance notice, it came to an end. That is, Boris and all the North Bucklore Symphony Orchestra members, except one, were apparently at the end of their evening's musical work.

Otto Knaap was not yet finished. All alone, superbly alone and quite unaware that his fellow volunteer musicians had reached the end of the work, he continued to pound away on the kettle drums, giving a new and quite unusual interpretation to Mr. Gustav Mahler's music. Conductor Boris, his face red as a beet, just stared at Otto.

Chas did not stare at Otto. He broke into a really loud and quite uncontrollable laugh, the same "ha, ha, ha", "hee, hee, hee" and "huu, huu, huu" laugh that caused the trouble during Reverend Heilig' s sermon about the mysterious Holy Trinity. Mr. George Smidge, who unfortunately happened to be sitting in the row immediately in front of the Lingoobers, turned around and glared at Chas as did about thirty other vultures for culture sitting in Glosky's Ballroom, which served as a concert hall for the Orchestra performance that evening.

Then Boris also turned around and shouted something really nasty at Chas, and the volunteer North Bucklore Symphony first violinist, or maybe, it was the volunteer second violinist, stood up and shook his bow in Chas's direction and, at the same instant, a North Bucklore culture vulture in the row behind the Lingoobers gave Chas a whack on the back of his head.

JUST THEN, CHAS AWOKE IN A COLD SWEAT!

Train of Thought

I lost my train of thought
the other day,
With no clue where it had
gone, or which way.

Thoughts of spring then
in my mind intruded,
Other flights of fancy interluded.

It was a welcome
respite for my brain,
Much better here than
with the missing train.

While I groped and
searched, words were
slow to come,
My facial expression,
rather blank and dumb.

Then in the distant haze
I viewed at last,
The lost train of thought
speeding from the past.

With luck I caught it
as it hurtled by,
Releasing flights of
fancy to the sky.

The DOUGH BOY

Chas Lingoober was nearly eight years old and thought he knew about all there was to know about most things. That is why Chas thought he knew everything one needed to know about making whole wheat bread.

Chas had often watched his Mom make bread. He knew that some whole wheat flour from Maurice Fuller, a little bit of salt, several cups of water, some sugar, and some other stuff were needed to make this type of bread. Oh, and don't forget the yeast! All these were mixed together in a very large bowl to create dough. Then that very large bowel with the dough inside was covered with a dish towel and left on the kitchen table. After a while, Chas was always amazed to see that the dough had risen so high that the dish towel had ballooned up over the top of the bowel. Then the real fun began! His Mom took off the towel and started punching the dough with her fists until the dough retreated back inside the bowel. She really used a lot of energy and exercised some weird facial expressions to beat the dough back into the bowel. The facial gyrations probably helped tame the dough.

Chas even knew where the whole wheat flour came from which was turned into whole bread. About once every other week, his Dad took Chas to visit a guy named Maurice Fuller. Maurice produced whole wheat flour which he put into bags and sold for $3.25 per bag to Chas's Dad. The label on each bag read: "Fuller's Flour Makes You Fuller".

Chas wished he had the $3.25 as pocket money to buy jaw breakers and metal clicker frogs at Buddha's, the local butcher shop, or perhaps several extra-large banana splits accompanied by a strawberry milkshake at Lehn's Ice Cream Shop. Both stores were located on Monroe Avenue, a short ride from the Lingoober home on Chas's metallic red Schwinn bicycle with the fat tires. On the handlebars of the bike was a horn that was operated by squeezing a large rubber hollow ball which resulted in a screeching ear-splitting yowling-type noise.

His Mom baked really tasty whole wheat bread. In the olden days, that is, in the 1950s, she made a big batch of this bread every Friday. A big batch produced about a half-dozen loaves of great smelling, brown crusted bread. Chas was always given one loaf to take to his third grade teacher, Mrs. Vinisch, who said nice things about the bread, about Chas's Mom and, once in a while, about Chas as well. The weekly loaf of fresh-out-of-the-oven whole wheat bread was helpful to move Chas, who was not a particularly bright or attentive scholar, from third to fourth grade at the local North Bucklore elementary school.

There was a time when Chas' Dad thought that he could make rye bread every bit as good as the whole wheat bread produced by his Mom. Unfortunately, his Dad's loaves of rye bread were hard as bricks which caused a lot of mirth in the Lingoober household.

He did not have a "bread-thumb". Someone suggested that the brick rye loaves could be sold to the local construction contractor for use in building new factory buildings. Well, today was Friday! By the time that Chas made his way to the kitchen, his Mom had already mixed the flour, salt, water, sugar and yeast into a huge batch of dough and placed it in the super large bowel on the kitchen table. A towel used to dry the dishes had taken its place on top of the bowel. And the towel had already begun to rise almost magically above the rim of the bowl!

Chas could hear his Mom talking on the phone with her good friend, Ruth. The subject matter of their telephone conversation was current events. The ladies expressed mutual astonishment at old Mrs. Mc Gellen's new hat, the one with the colourful vegetable garden on its top. She was something of a sensation around town because she drove a 1938 six-cylinder yellow Packard with a maroon coloured convertible top. The Packard had been previously owed by one of Mrs. Mc Gellen's three long deceased husbands. Mrs. Mc Gellen apparently never fully learned how to shift from one Packard gear to another with the result that from blocks away it was possible to hear the grinding battle of stick shift, clutch and transmission as she tried to move from first into second gear.

Chas' Mom and her friend, Ruth, then moved into a thorough discussion of a shocking event involving two teenage neighbour boys.

They were recently caught by North Bucklore's finest, that is the local cops, drinking beer and brandy on the local Town And Country golf course. The good ladies on the telephone worked themselves up into nearly righteous anger over the shame that these under-age boys had brought to their neighbourhood.

Apparently the older of the two boys, John Marot by name, had somewhere (possibly at the Biker Bar located across the street from the Courthouse) purchased a very cheap grade of brandy, known in the local parlance, as "gut rot", even though he was underage and therefore legally forbidden from doing so. The younger chap, Jan Burdick, also known as "Fat Duff" in the neighbourhood, had contributed to the occasion by "borrowing" a six-pack of Hamm's Beer from his Dad. By the way, no-one called Jan, who weighed in at 210 pounds, "Fat Duff" to his face, because to do so would mean several weeks in St. Vincent's hospital.

Mrs. Gossum, the local snitch with purple-dyed hair and a face full of wrinkles, had reported the boys to the police. Her eagle eyes had spotted them on the golf course as she was walking her fat dachshund, Cindy, near the 17th hole. Acting on the snitch's breathless telephone call, six of North Bucklore's finest police officers sped to the golf course in three squad cars, where the petty crime was taking place. In true law and order fashion, they surrounded the surprised and not just a little frightened John and Jan and hustled them into a squad car for a free ride to the police department.

The police car was a chunky, not very fast, black 1952 Ford with a red rotating bubble light on the top. The police could not refrain from turning on the bubble light and the siren, as well, as the boys were chauffeured from the place of the crime to police station located behind the North Bucklore Courthouse. The desk sergeant, who was in charge of paperwork regarding this incident, wished that he had never met the boys who had been arrested for trespassing on the Town And Country Gulf Course. Jan, with a thunderous belch, threw up about a pint of cheap brandy and beer mingled with pretzel residue on the staff sergeant's desk with splatters on his white starched shirt and blue clip-on tie. Ruth and Chas' Mom would spend at least another half hour on the John and Jan drama.

Chas had an idea. He would speed up the bread-making process by punching down the dough while his Mom was on the telephone with Ruth. He was certain his Mom would be mighty pleased with this initiative. Chas also figured his planned work on the bread would help get him out of the dog-house where he had landed several weeks ago when his attempt to fix his Mom's cuckoo clock failed miserably.

The clock was a wedding present to his parents from his mother's dear Aunt Edna. The dumb cuckoo bird in the clock popped out of its house twelve minutes after the hour, rather than exactly on the hour, like every normal cuckoo clock. Because Chas, being now nearly eight years old,

thought he knew how to do everything, it was no problem for him to believe that he could fix that clock which came from a place in Germany called the Dark Forest or Black Forest or Slack Boris, or something like that. Just as he took the clock from the wall while standing on a wobbly piece of furniture, the clock went flying through the air and landed on the floor in very many pieces. Chas himself landed on the floor as well; actually he landed on his head on the floor.

In the Lingoober household, there was a strict rule that no-one, without exception, was allowed to step or stand on the furniture. The cuckoo clock disaster occurred in large part because Chas disobeyed this rule. In the kitchen, the table on which the very large bowl of rising whole wheat dough was located and the chairs around the table were included as furniture, on which Chas was neither to climb or stand. This absolute rule did not stop Chas Lingoober from pushing a chair close to the kitchen table, climbing on the chair, then stepping from the chair onto the table where he stood in front of the huge bowel filled with high rise dough covered by a dish towel.

Chas felt more than just a little giddy and anxious standing on the forbidden table. Actually, the table had nothing forbidden about it, but his standing on the table was totally forbidden. He cautiously looked around from on high at the kitchen cabinets painted cream colour with red trim, the sink located under the window looking out at his Mom's mock orange bushes.

Chas could never understand why those scraggly bushes were called mock orange, since they never produced anything that even faintly resembled oranges.

He also spied the ice-box. Yes, that squat white cabinet with the nearly continuously humming motor at its backside was actually called an ice-box, probably, because it made trays of ice-cubes in addition to its main duty of keeping milk, vegetables, cheese and other perishable food chilled. Chas's Dad said that in the really olden days, the ice-box had no motor to keep its interior cool. Instead, a big chunk of ice was placed on the top of the cabinet and that functioned as the cooling mechanism.

And talking of milk, a man called a "milk-man" delivered gallon glass bottles of milk, with about two inches of cream at the top of each bottle, to the Lingoober household at least three times a week. The name of the milk distributor was Verifine and the milk-man delivering the Verifine gallon bottles of milk wore bib overalls and a cap with a brim on it. He also delivered cottage cheese, if his customer wanted some of that very fine product. The gallon bottles of milk were placed by this milk-man in a "milk-chute"which was an opening in the wall near the rear door of the Lingoober house. This opening had a metal door which the milk-man opened to place the milk bottles in, then closed so the milk could not get out.

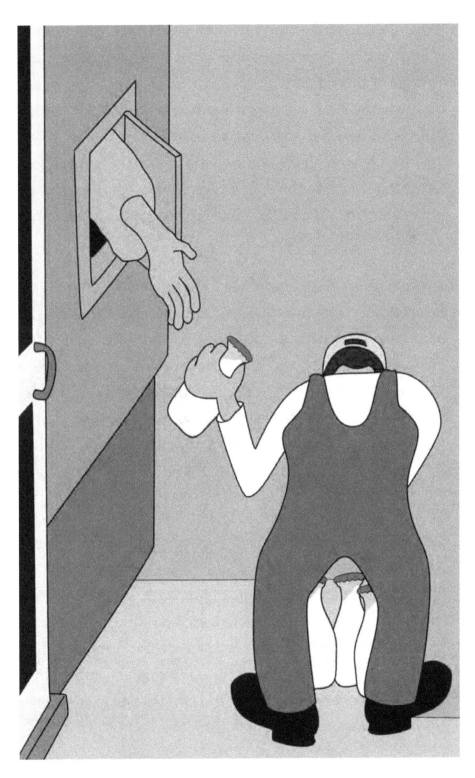

There was another door to the milk-chute on the inside of house that allowed his Mom, often while still in her nightgown and slippers, to remove the milk from the chute for use in the kitchen during breakfast or for storage in the ice-box. And by the way, Chas sometimes climbed through the milk-chute to enter and exit the Lingoober household, rather than using the back door, like a young gentleman was supposed to do. Of course, crawling through the milk-chute was also strictly forbidden.

It was only last week that Chas tried to help by removing a gallon of milk from the chute and taking it into the kitchen, where the darn bottle slipped out his grasp and crashed to the floor. That created a hullaballoo, what with a gallon of milk and cream running under the ice-box and under the stove and under the kitchen table and everywhere else and smithereens of glass spread far and wide.

Chas squatted down on his knees with the dough bowel between his legs. He carefully removed the cloth thereby revealing the awesome dough puffing out over the rim of the bowel. He balled each hand into a fist and raised his arms high over the dough, sort of like Maestro Shanski, the conductor of the North Bucklore Symphony Orchestra, when he is about to start the orchestra in the performance of a long and difficult piece by a famous German or Russian or Finnish composer. Chas screwed up his face into a menacing grimace and after a short pause punched his fists into

the dough. His punch was so energetic and so successful that his fists were propelled to the very bottom of the bowel. He was amazed to realize that not only his fists were buried in the dough, but his arms nearly up to his armpits were also buried in the stuff. It was now at this rather late point in time that Chas discovered the super stickiness of the dough. He tried to move his arms, but the heavy gluey dough held him fast. Instead of freeing his arms, he just moved the bowel to one side of the table. Chas was smart enough to know that he had a problem, indeed a serious problem, but he was not clever enough to know exactly how to free himself. The more he attempted to move his arms in the dough, the more he moved the bowel around the table. He leaned over the bowel and, in a panic, attempted to pull his right arm out of the bowel. Then it happened! The huge pottery bowel, the huge sticky mass of whole wheat dough and a very frightened Chas whose arms were still deep in the dough all fell off the table. When the bowel hit the kitchen floor, it broke into a million pieces and Chas landed head-first in the pile of dough. Just as everything went black, he heard his Mom's high pitched, warbling scream.

Two seconds after this frightful
event, Chas awoke in a...

COLD SWEAT!

The BONEL PRIZE for LITURATURE

Clem Hupfenstock was informed by an old fashioned land line telephone call that he was the honourable nominee of the distinguished Bonel Prize for Fine Literature. That was good because Clem, a real tech dummy, did not own a cell phone. The person who made this dramatic call was Erich Wittlesdinger, that is: Professor Erich Wittlesdinger, the Chairman of the North Bucklore Literary And Social Club, also known as the NBLSC. It was fashionable to make the call to the Prize recipient late at night in order to add to its drama which is the reason why a very surprised Clem Hupfenstock took the phone call at 11:08 in the evening of Saturday, March 15th, 1999. Actually, his wife, Hilda, initially took the call and in a very giddy voice ordered Clem to the phone.

To understand the importance of the Bonel Prize, it is useful to become acquainted with the North Bucklore Literary And Social Club. Glosky's Tavern was the place where the Club was born. The auspicious date was Monday, June 10th, 1994 and the parents of the Club were a number of North Bucklore drinking buddies with Eddy Bolen as the ring-leader. Those buddies included Peter Zahn, the one and only dentist in town; Chuck Sharkey, a senior partner of the two-man law firm of Getum & Sharkey; Heinrich Leib, who was the local undertaker; and Gus Jeckley, the proprietor of the Bucklore Finer Pre-Owned Car Emporium.

Eddy was the founder and President of Bonel Kitchen Improvement Products Incorporated and the proud inventor of a new type of vegetable chopping and shredding machine, known as the VCS Machine which was available in better department stores in New England. Unfortunately for Eddy, the VCS Machine was based on patented technology that did not belong to him, a fact which came home to roost about ten years later when he was sued successfully for big bucks by the rightful owner of the technology, causing Eddy and his wife Rose Mary to seek the protection of the bankruptcy courts. But in 1994, and particularly on June 10th of that year, everything looked mighty rosy for Eddy Bonel and he was quite happy to be a big shot in little North Bucklore.

Inspired by more than a few shots of Red Rooster brandy followed by more than a few glasses of Hamm's Beer – which was advertised to come from the Land of Sky Blue Waters, Eddy dramatically announced, out of the blue, that there should be a literary club in North Bucklore. The announcement initially produced nothing more than glassy stares from his drinking buddies who did not quite understand what Eddy was talking about. Amid a series of beer belly belches, Eddy pointed out that many neighbouring towns had an organization where local poets and writers, or those who thought they could be classified as poets or writers, could gather and amuse one another with their genius and talent.

In particular, Sobiesky Corners, which was looked down on by all well-informed North Bucklorers, was the proud gathering place of the Sobiesky Corners Poets and Writers Association of the United States of America. It was appropriate that North Bucklore had its very own literary club, or so said Eddy.

The germ of the club idea may have come from Eddy's attempt during his Senior year at North Bucklore High School to write an epic poem about a Seneca Indian (now called, Native American) princess who saved several families of settlers from starvation in 1790. Eddy was not very successful at this attempt, being only able to complete about a dozen lines of the epic poem. Confusing the idea with reality, Eddy thought of himself as a writer of great and dramatic epic poems. He also prided himself as being a descendant of a Seneca Indian Chief, which heritage was the direct result of Eddy's over-active imagination. Eddy's dad informed Eddy that their name originally was Bolensky, which was of Polish origin, without the slightest trace of Indian nobility.

After Eddy bought a few rounds of Red Rooster brandy for his buddies, each round followed, of course, by a Hamm's beer chaser, they warmed up to his idea of a literary club for North Bucklore. In fact, Chuck Sharkey, the local lawyer who fantasized the club as a potential new client, got off his bar stool and raised his glass of brandy in a toast to the new club. To tell the truth, Chuck made this toast while standing

on a Glosky's Tavern bar stool. So the North Bucklore Literary And Social Club, otherwise known as NBLSC, was born with Eddy Bolen, Peter Zahn, Chuck Sharkey, Heinrich Leib and Gus Jeckley as the distinguished founding members.

Clem Hupfenstock, Adjunct Professor of Business Ethics and Responsibility at the branch of the state university located in North Bucklore, did not consider himself much of a poet. The poem that had attracted the attention of the North Bucklore Literary and Social Club and which was considered to be of a sufficiently high literary quality to win the Bonel Prize in 1999 had the un-inspiring and un-imaginative title "The Jogger and the Leaf". About six months ago, Clem's wife, Hilda, had spotted this piece of second-rate literature on Clem's desk while she was doing her daily snooping into her husband's private affairs. Hilda read the poem and liked it, although she had a hard time believing that Clem possessed the talent to write what she considered to be very clever verses. Without informing her husband, Hilda submitted the poem to the NBLSC as a great work of her husband to be considered for the prestigious Bonel Prize.

As its title suggested, the banal subject matters of the poem were a jogger and a leaf:

While jogging on a city street,
I heard a flutter at my feet,
And looking down while keeping stride,
Borne on the wind a leaf I spied.

That leaf had a force of its own,
Like me on a run alone.
On its course it never tarried,
Steadily on a light breeze carried

In daring challenge then to me,
From ties of nature somehow free,
It picked up speed and passed me by,
Skittering on the breeze, set to fly.

I watched that leaf more than amazed,
As on the breeze it turned and swayed.
With grace and ease gently rocking,
Floating past, my presence mocking.

As it passed I quickened my pace,
Determined with that leaf to race.
Though its advantage was unfair,
'Cause it, not I, could float on air.

Who would have known that during this run,
I'd meet this strange phenomenon.
A leaf which a new life had found
In this town now racing around.

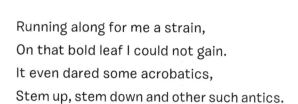

Running along for me a strain,
On that bold leaf I could not gain.
It even dared some acrobatics,
Stem up, stem down and other such antics.

Its autumn colours shown in the sun,
T'was clear for it the race was fun.
That leaf in blissful gyration,
But for me just agitation.

So in my mind I set a goal,
Several blocks farther near the pole.
This crazy race would find its end,
The winner being determined then.

Surely now between here and there,
That leaf would get hung up somewhere.
Or, make a sharp turn with a slight swirl,
And into a bush lightly twirl.

Fast approaching the finish line,
The leaf ahead, me still behind.
With great effort and some more speed,
I could then pass and take the lead.

But t'was the wind, a strong ally,
Moving that leaf faster than I.
With a skitter and a flurry,
First 'cross the line in a hurry.

And spiralling then up and away,
Colors shimm'ring in light of day,
That darn leaf was skyward bound
With me flat-footed on the ground.

Even an amateur would know that this poem did not deserve a prize of any kind whatsoever. It was stupid to imagine that a leaf would somehow race with a two-legged human being. It was also impossible to imagine that Clem Hupfenstock, Adjunct Professor of Ethics And Responsibility, with more than two hundred-twenty pounds on his short human frame, ever went jogging. Leaves fall from trees to the ground and stay there until they are raked into piles. Kids jump into the piles and scatter the leaves around. That's about it.

The big Bonel prize day was set for August 23, 1999. Clem rented a black tuxedo with a red clip-on bow tie. The trousers required some renovations in order to fit Clem's rotund figure. He was not particularly concerned that nothing seemed to fit properly. That was because no clothes ever fit properly on Clem.

Hilda, Clem's wife, bought a dark green velvety dress from the local consignment shop. Her plan was to bring it back to the shop for a full cash refund after the Bolen Prize event on the grounds that it did not fit. The green dress on Hilda's skinny, bony frame was a visual improvement. A visit to a beauty salon to do something about her wispy greying hair would have also been a great help. But Hilda decided she did not need the help of a hair dresser and so arrived at the event looking like she indeed needed the help of a hair dresser. The distinguished Bonel Prize for Fine Literature was to be awarded to Professor Clem Hupfenstock at a dinner to be held at Glosky's Ballroom, which was decorated with blue and green streamers, plastic dwarf palm trees and a large framed likeness of the honourable Prize winner. The picture of Clem showed him looking mighty serious, very much like an Adjunct Professor. His sparse light brown hair was combed over smartly from the left side of his head across the top where he was quite bald over to the right side of his head. Unlike in the photo showing his hairdo unchanging and in near perfect order, in real life his left side hair had a mind of its own and refused to stay combed over to the right side. The result was somewhat comical with all the extra-long left side hair hanging down over his left ear. Some folks who observed this situation thought that Clem's hair disorder was simply a typical professorial "thing", for lack of a better term, and a sign of great intelligence.

All the important citizens of North Bucklore and some not so important characters streamed into the Ballroom between 6:00 and 6:30 where they enjoyed free *RIPPLE* sparkling wine served in red plastic cups and a free selection of tiny sausages, crackers smeared with liverwurst from a liverwurst manufacturer in Sheboygan, Wisconsin, radishes and candied pickles from up-state New York.

Those in attendance included, of course, the founding fathers of the North Bucklore Literary and Social Club, and the other members of the Club. Also present were most of the members of the Buffalo Club, many of whom were also members of the NBLSC. Looking around, one could spy Messieurs Eddy Bolen, Peter Zahn, Chuck Sharkey, Heinrich Leib and Gus Jeckley and their respective wives or girl-friends. Also the Honorable George Smidge and his wife, Booty, were present. The entire show was directed by Professor Erich Wittlesdinger, Honorable President of the Club who looked mighty important in tuxedo and patent leather shoes and who was very busy greeting all the guests.

Even the Reverend Karl Benedictus was in attendance and looking forward to a free meal. His main function would be to present an invocation, that is, his job would be to request the blessing of the supernatural on everyone and everything in Glosky's Ballroom that evening. The good Reverend greatly enjoyed the liverwurst crackers, so much so, that he took two at a time, many times. The sparkly wine was also to his

liking, being a few grades higher than the Mass wine usually available in St. Wilhelmina's Church.

Clem in his somewhat ill-fitting tuxedo and Hilda in her velvety green dress were all smiles as they followed Professor Wittlesdinger to the head table. The guests took their seats. Reverend Benedictus was also seated at the main table as were Eddy Bolen and his wife, Edwina, and other notables, including, of course, Professor Wittlesdinger and his current girlfriend, Mary Beth Goronski, the local librarian who also was a competitive roller skater.

Karl Benedictus used the paper napkin at his place to wipe some liverwurst off his hands. He had accidentally placed one of the many liverwurst crackers that he met that evening up-side down in his right hand with the result that his right palm was covered with wurst. So were the right palms of those guests with whom he shook hands, much to their amazement and annoyance. But it was not appropriate to complain to the Reverend, due to his alleged close contact with the Almighty.

It was just at that moment when a man with a most noticeable scowl on his bearded face entered the ball-room. He was at least six feet tall and was wearing a black and white checkered jacket over what looked like a multi-colored lumberjack's shirt. His trousers were of a dull yellow color and his footwear was of the kind available at the local tractor supply store. He looked around until he spied the smiling and affable Professor Wittlesdinger.

He then proceeded to make his way to the main table where the Professor was about to sit down. The scowling intruder pulled the Professor to one side, somewhat away from the table. The two men were engaged for several minutes in earnest and animated conversation about what appeared to be the contents of several pieces of paper that the stranger had pulled out of his pocket and shown to Wittlesdinger. A deep scowl now replaced the smile on the face of the Professor who glanced in the direction of Clem Hupfenstock.

The stranger was none other than Fritz Dodder who was none other than the Chairman of the Sobiesky Corners Poets and Writers Association. What in heck was Mr. Dodder doing at the Bonel Prize event? He certainly had not been invited. Well, everyone present found out why Mr. Dodder was there when Professor Wittlesdinger walked over to the microphone and made the following announcement:

"Ladies and Gentlemen, I am annoyed, perturbed and irritated to have to inform you that Mr. Clem Hupfenstock is not the author of The Jogger and the Leaf poem and does not deserve the Bonel Prize. I have just received convincing evidence proving that Mr. Hupfenstock plagiarized this piece of literature from a member of the Sobiesky Corners Poets and Writers Association, whose name I am not free to divulge at this time. This distressing news about this despicable act of plagiarism gives me no choice but to cancel this event ..."

At this point the Chairman of the NBLSC was interrupted by a loud wail morphing into a scream coming from Hilda Hupfenstock who then proceeded to fall off her chair onto the floor in a dead faint. She managed to pull on top of her as she collapsed onto the floor the tablecloth and ten place settings plus a large vase of flowers that served as a centrepiece on the table as well as an assortment of glasses filled with various amounts of sparkling wine.

Adjunct Professor Clem'sface turned beet red as he listened to the Chairman Wittlesdinger's announcement. He had indeed neglected to inform the NBLSC that the Jogger and the Leaf poem was not conceived or written by him. In fact, he had never written a single line of verse, good or bad, in his life. Huge drops of sweat appeared on his chubby beet-coloured face while his left side hair which had been somewhat neatly combed over to the right side of his bald head fell of its own accord back over and well below his left ear and he felt an awful pain in his chest.

About three seconds after this hair incident and feeling the chest pain, Clem awoke in a ...

COLD SWEAT!

CPSIA information can be obtained
at www.ICGtesting.com
Printed in the USA
BVHW030858160623
666010BV00003B/751